THE ' RICH' RENEGADE

THE BOOK THAT WON'T MAKE YOU RICH.

MINO PLANTS

Copyright © Mino Plants
All Rights Reserved.

This book has been published with all efforts taken to make the material error-free after the consent of the author. However, the author and the publisher do not assume and hereby disclaim any liability to any party for any loss, damage, or disruption caused by errors or omissions, whether such errors or omissions result from negligence, accident, or any other cause.

While every effort has been made to avoid any mistake or omission, this publication is being sold on the condition and understanding that neither the author nor the publishers or printers would be liable in any manner to any person by reason of any mistake or omission in this publication or for any action taken or omitted to be taken or advice rendered or accepted on the basis of this work. For any defect in printing or binding the publishers will be liable only to replace the defective copy by another copy of this work then available.

The Novel is dedicated to my family who helped during the writing period.

Contents

Preface

I got the idea for this novella when I was in 7th grade and was in boarding school. I just foreshadowed it and wrote it when I was at home. Hey, I am Akshit[Pen Name, Mino Plants]. My age is 13 and I know that's quite a small age. But I don't know when I show this Novel to someone else, he/she thinks I am in my early 20s. Well I won't say much, cause paper is made of trees, and I want to save the nature.

Acknowledgements

Well, first big thanks to Notion Press for letting me complete my Novel. Second, thanks to my sister who gave true opinions and told me where it needed improvement. And lastly, thanks to my imagination.

Prologue

'I was stabbed 5 times in the stomach by my family, I still survived somehow. I was black. The place we lived in, Yuingo, had just whites. I took a flight, consulted an agent, and rented a flat, here in Sorum. Didn't have any job, had a difficult life, had to strive for food. And then I found this guy called Pill. He took me to many clubs and bars and then I just lived on beers. I told him everything, we became good friends, and most importantly, Sorum didn't promote racism like Yuingo. Pill is a great friend. I have to bend down a few centimeters to stare into his eyes. He eats a lot. Sometimes, he would bring me his donuts. And sometimes, he would give me some money. My family would find me, break into my house and take everything away. I never had a father's love nor a mother's love. Pill was very fond of his parents. Whenever I saw him, it made me cry. Those tears watered the plant of happiness.' read the diary page of Scott Langs' journal.

CHAPTER ONE

Sorum's Fate

HNO 24, Floor 14, Amaro Flats, Sorum city:

An untidy room scattered with clothes and socks. The couch was half ripped. On the table next to the couch was a pile of beer bottles. The only light in the room was coming from the glitched television. A person named Scott was lying on the couch with a beer bottle in his hand. The television showed nothing but created an ' electric hum' which he surely was enjoying. He had a short beard which didn't match with his drunkard behavior. He was thin but still was powerful. Anyone new would surely think that he has a mental breakdown. He could drink 8 bottles in a row! But that's normal in the city he lives in. Sorum was full of clubs and bars and local liquor shops. In the day, the Sun's rays would be blocked by tall swaying buildings, and when the Moon would show its ' potholed ' face, the roads would be full of cars. The palm trees would be decorated with pink and blue lights. The bars would open. Even teens would go and have tons of alcohol. The nights were the real deal in Sorum.

Thedoorbell rang." Oh!, now who's here to meet me?" murmured Scott in an exhausted voice. He got up, wore his vest which had holes in it, went to the door, and opened it.

"Hello is this Scott?" said a well-dressed man, confused. He was with 2 or 3 people and all of them were greatly dressed. They all looked pretty much similar. All had long beards. " Uhm, yeah this is Scott Langs," said Scott feeling embarrassed." Are we at the wrong place?" whispered the man to his group member." Yeah, this is my friend," came the reply from the member.

The man came back to Scott and said" There's no time to chit-chat okay? Let me tell you who we are. We are 'United', and we finish crime in the city. I am Trent, the leader of this group. Meet Ivan, Joel, and your friend Pill. Now we need you to work with us on a crime that has been going on for 1 year. Our group will finish it quickly and get 1000 pepri." " Man, I don't need any paper," replied Scott though he had no money.

Ivan had a cut on his eyebrow which he had gotten during a gunfight. He had a ginger mohawk haircut. Some bullets were attached to his bag and had a pistol every time. Joel had short hair from the sides. He had some wrinkles under his eyes. Trent was same as Joel but had nasolabial folds.

"Think about it. You can buy a thousand beer bottles," Joel said.

Scott now started thinking deeply. Pill came forward and whispered," we have two piles at the office. C'mon." "Okay, I'll go with you. Y'all go back to the office and I'll be there soon. Just tell me the address."

"We'll be expecting you. Boys, let's go." The door bangs and they leave. Scott gets back to his couch, lies down, and grabs another bottle. "Another mess to deal with. My life is full of terrible consequences. I'm just trashed up." He gets up, wears a shirt, gets out of his heavenly world, and grabs a taxi.

United Spire, Sorum City:

"Where your man at, Pill?" asked Trent frustrated.

"At the washroom probably due to inflammation of his stomach," came the reply. The office wasn't like any other building. It was small but still looked luxurious. There were two messed-up circles on the table. Everything was made of glass. It was all Trent's giving. He had solved many cases and had won thousands of pepri. Trent was intelligent, a good fighter and that's why everybody loved him, either at the office or in Sorum.

" Boss, our guy is here," informed Ivan." What took you so long my friend? We were waiting for you." interrogated Trent. Yes, he was angry but he couldn't scream at him or he would leave work. Trent was an experienced guy. He knew how to handle newbies." I don't know. After you left, I too left my home in 10 minutes. And probably it would take 15 minutes to reach here. I would be here by 30 minutes, but somehow it took an hour. I don't know," replied Scott while he was looking at his own whole body." Hey, you still tipsy?" asked Joel smirkingly. " Yes, I am but I will understand whatever you'll say," responded Scott.

"Hey enough. We've done much talking. So Scott Langs, your friend here told us that you are a tough guy and you could assist us in catching a criminal who is associated with the massacre of innumerable people. So Pill, would you please show us on the TV?" Trent spake. Pill went to the switch, turned it on, right-swiped on its screen, and went back." Scott, this is the criminal and his name is Mica," Trent said but in a low-pitched voice. Mica wore a black-colored jacket of leather, a black winter cap, a black balaclava, and a digital goggle that read death. His face was barely visible. That's why it was more difficult to catch him." We don't know his face. We don't know his base.

We just know his name," said Joel. " And that's why we have hired you Scott Langs. It's not just about money, it's about all those innocent people who were killed by this man." After Trent said this line, he was looking like a hero. Everybody looked at Langs, but he was not there." Ah!! Where did he go? Did he even listen to us?" said Trent angrily. He never got angry but this time he was." I think he's at the washroom," said Ivan." That's so unprofessional of him," said Joel to his boss. 2 minutes went and there was complete silence. Pill broke the silence and said," Hey, there he is."

Scott still looked puzzled." Hey man, you are getting unprofessional. Next time be prepared. Did you even listen to what we said?" questioned Trent.

" Uhmm, yeah, I heard. You told the criminal was Mica and I even looked at him. He was all black. He wasn't a racist." This line said by Scott made angry Trent laugh. " You got a great sense of humor," said Ivan. They all sat at the dining table. It was very awkward.

" Okay, back to the plan. Now, Sorum is a big city. It will be extremely difficult to find Mica. We all will suggest ideas and choose the correct one," said Joel. " Okay, Scott we'll start with you. What are your opinions?" Trent said. Scott takes a sip from the beer and says "Okay, I've got an idea but it doesn't seem to be working. How 'bout 'we' kill people?"

Pill was furious about this. " Are you out of your mind? What trash are you talking about?"

" Just listen. We 'kill' people and gain Mica's trust. And then at the right time, we strike him. We will be the ' Rich Renegade'.

Everybody thought about this plan. " But we can't kill people." Trent doubted. Scott laughed and said" Who is gonna kill people? We will fake the death. Now listen, one of us will pretend to kill all of us. Trent, do we have any other group that we can work with?"

" We have an enemy group called 'Bangers', should I call them?" jabbered Pill scoffingly" Not now, and this fake killing can probably gain Mica's faith," Scott said bending a bit towards the table.

Ivan thought for some time. Then catechized," That's a wonderful plan, but what's the problem then?"

" The only problem is that we don't know when and where should we perform it," Scott said sadly.

" Well, so our priority should be knowing when and where?" answered Joel.

" Exactly." came the reply from Scott. Trent thought of testing Scott's intelligence. He asked him" Well if we can find where he is, then what is the use of doing all this drama? We'll go and catch him. No need of gaining trust." Everybody agreed with Trent. " That's a good question there Mr. Trent. But remember, Mica is much stronger, more intelligent, fast, and smarter than us. We might be killed too. And we want this to work with ease. We will gather information about him. Maybe there could be 2 Micas or maybe he could be working for somebody. That's why we need to play smart. Any doubts?" Scott quickly replied. Everybody stood up and gave him a round of applause. Trent was finally impressed by Scott. This Scott was different from the Scott in Amaro Flats. " The... meeting is dismissed. You all can go and rest now," Scott ordered. Pill replied," But, it's only been ten minutes." " Don't argue, 'kay? Joel, you stay here," came the reply from Trent. Pill walked to his home, Ivan went by car, and Scott took a taxi.

It was 5:00 PM now and the orange rays were striking Trent's miserable face. Trent was a tough guy, but robust

guys do cry. And now Trent was an example of it."
Brother?" Trent asked Joel." We have been through tough
times. We both suffered it. And you know? This is the
mystery I want to complete. I wanna get that 'asesino' and
I'll not kill him, but I'll torment him, torture him every
single day!" Trent's voice was shaky, his throat was heavy.
"That guy killed my daughter. He killed my wife. He killed
my familia! And now I have you. And I don't want to..."
Trent hugged him." Hey, hermano, don't! We'll surely get
him. We'll get our revenge. Comprendo?" Joel assured him
though his voice was also getting heavy. Trent wiped away
his tears." Adios hermano!" Trent said, took a taxi, and went
back to his apartment.

Samira: Hey daddy, come let's play!

Trent: C'mon daughter, but it's getting late. We'll have
to sleep early or a persona loca will come and pick you up
and kidnap you.

Samira: [laughs] Daddy, I am 5 years old now. I ain't
afraid of anyone.

Trent: Yes! That's my girl.

Laura: Trent, Samira, it's going to rain. Both of you come
back.

Trent: Hey little one, wanna have a ride on my back?[
Samira jumps on his back] Ooh! You getting heavy!

Samira: Quit it! I ain't fat. Ricochet is 25 kg.

Trent: He is in 2nd class.

[Trent slides the glass door]

Samira: Mommarooney! I'm hungry.

Trent: I'm hungry too!

Laura: Hey, you guys just ate two bowls of ramen 10
minutes ago. C'mon, let's sleep. It won't make you hungry.
I'll make churros tomorrow.

Samira: Pops, it started raining outside.[lightning strikes]

Trent: Okay, I'm turning off the lights.[Everybody lies on the bed]

[Trent feels a harsh touch on his face]

Trent: [opens his eyes] Samira?! Laura?! Where are they both?[gets up from his bed and turns the light on] Ah!! Light's gone.[starts walking towards the hall] Where have they gone?[A man catches Trent from his throat]

Mica: Hey! I'm Mica.[grabs his knife and stabs it on his thigh]

Trent: No! Ah! mierda![falls to the ground] Hey! You! Where are my daughter and my wife?!

[Mica leaves the house. A flash of lightning strikes providing enough light so that Trent could see Samira and Laura.]

Trent:[sees Samira and Laura covered with blood]

Trent woke up with sudden jerks." Huh! It was all just a memory." This was the first sentence that was blurted out by Trent. He put aside his blanket and went straight to the window. It was raining outside. The palm trees decorated with the lights looked exquisite. He looked at the sky and for the first time, he was feeling relaxed. For the first time, he felt that his city was glorious.' I think I should have played in the rain with Samira,' One bogey of Trent's train of thought derailed. The noise because of the derailing was so loud that even the Moon closed its ears. Everything around him was like Paradise. And he was fully energized for his day. And he was sure that the culprit was near. His thigh was being massaged too, by his cellphone."Oh! Who is it now? Ivan!" It was surprising because the clock struck 3:00 in the morning. He picked it up," Hello Ivan! What happened?!"

" Hey, I've heard that the taxi Scott was in, that was going to Caruom club crashed."

" Oh my! Call Joel and Pill and I'll see you there," Trent's heaven again changed back into a normal world.

CHAPTER TWO

Deliberate Mistake

" Oh my god! Get them out," Joel screamed as he saw the taxi's condition. Taxi's glasses were broken. It was squeezed from the front. They opened its doors and saw that the driver was stabbed in her neck and Scott was also stabbed in his stomach. The mirror was shattered and its debris was stuck on the driver's neck."Hey, c'mon wake up Scott! Scott! Shit! Call an ambulance," The taxi driver had a brutal death. His eyes were open because of the sudden impact. They checked his body and found just the stabbing point on the neck." Pill, identify with what object he has been stabbed with," Trent commanded." He was stabbed with a pocket knife. It's a damn murder." "We can't lose him, should I take him in my car?" asked Ivan. " No need, there is the ambulance. C'mon let's load him up, he is a priority to us, "Trent informed. Scott's treatment caused 500 pepri. They reached the hospital." Leave it on me. I'll pay for him," said Trent because Langs reminded him of his daughter. 5 minutes later, the doctor came with a pocketknife in his hand and said," It was dug down deep in the victim's stomach." Pill took the knife, wore his large gloves, and rubbed the knife." Trent, the knife has something written," Pill handed over the knife to Trent. The knife had a skeleton bijou. The knife read ' Angora,

Mica'. " What does it read?" Ivan interrogated. Trent was mute. He rolled his pants and then measured the tip of the knife with his scar. He was now sure." Guys, The person is Mica. And he is calling us to Angora,"

Joel was confused." Why in the heck does he want us?" The situation was becoming tense. " There is a 70% chance that he is working for someone. And the person he's working for probably has enmity with us. That's why he wants us. And it'll not be easy. I think we're going to bite the bullet," Trent declared.

Pill saw the situation and tried to make everybody laugh." Hey, but it's damn easy to bite a bullet. I've seen it in movies. The villain shoots the hero, and the hero catches it with his teeth!" Trent was angry and Pill's statement made the situation worse." Hey, who brought this guy to our group, that guy is fired!" Trent furiously said. Ivan replied," It was you, Boss!" Trent tried to change the topic," Hey, let's ask the doctor about Scott. Then, with Scott, we will continue our journey." Pill's statement made the situation a bit better. Pill had succeeded in his plan. They waited for an hour, then the doctor came back with the reports." I'm sorry, but it will take 15 days to recover fully." Trent blurted out," We have a home doctor, Dr. Pill, he'll take care of him."

The doctor was still not convinced. After arguing, the doctor was convinced but he still warned Trent." He should not be taking any mental or physical stress." "Surely, but what else does the report say?" came the reply. The doctor put on his glasses, and looked carefully at the report." We are not sure but we think he is mentally ill. He. So you have to keep him packed up. And best of luck on your mission Trent."

" Thanks, doctor. You don't need to worry about Scott."

Angora City, Southside trench, Tricky's open bar.

Angora city, the city completely different from Sorum. Angora city was often known as ' The Monsoon City'. The petrichor, the waterfalls, and the Latin-American houses built on mountains looked exquisite. The sun's rays would strike the mountains and the place would look serene. But at night, no light would be turned on, just a few homes. The beaches didn't have people, but only sand lying supine. The city was deserted. Or the people were killed by Mica. ' United' was at the beach at an open bar. Joel was leisurely supporting himself with the bar stand. Trent was having a cocktail, Scott was sitting on the bench, and Ivan had kept his chin on his hand and his eyes were puffed. Scott got up, went to Ivan, and said," Hey, you got clinomania or something?" Ivan was alarmed," Wow! That word is making me more sleepy? Do you think you can fight me over beautiful words?! How 'bout ' Pluviophile'?"

" What does it even mean?"

Ivan raised his eyebrow," I don't care what it means. I am the best teacher! Yes!!" Scott's lips widen a bit," Man, you are still inebriated."

Ivan raised his second eyebrow," Another beautiful word."

" Shut up!" Scott said in a low voice because he saw Trent concentrate on something. Ivan's eyebrow came down," Another one." He then started laughing and fell.

" What happened to him?" Joel asked. Scott chuckled and said," He's just...passed away. Let him sleep."

A car drifted on the beach, throwing sand on Ivan's figure. The gates opened and Pill came out. He was worried," Negative, just 5 people." Trent got up quickly," That's not right. Joel, go and find what's going on in this city." Trent chose Joel because Joel was good with social interactions. Joel went on to the upward slanting road watching every house. He looked on every roof and one house was the destination. He saw Mica sitting on the roof with his laptop. Mica looked at Joel and mocked him by showing with signs' I am ready. Come, let's have some fun.' Joel retreated a few steps back, opened his radio talky, and said," Guys, I'm in front of the devil. I'm chasing him. If I'll need help, I'll drop a flare." Back at the bar, Scott informed everybody as he only had the radio talky." Joel's a tough guy. He won't need our help." Trent assured.

Joel started running after him. Mica was still sitting. When Joel was on the same roof as Mica, he smirked and jumped off to the road. Joel also jumped. They were standing face to face. Mica backed a bit," Hey, you are a big guy. I don't think you can catch up with me." Joel immediately said," Don't judge a book by its cover." Mica again leered and said," That's a cliche. So no more talks. And catch me if you can." A van passed at a high speed in front of Mica. And when it passed Mica was gone. Joel ran towards the van. He suddenly stopped chasing it. A hand came out from the alley and pulled Joel in. " Now let's have a good fight." Mica declared.

CHAPTER THREE

Witnessing Brawl

They both stared at each other, though Mica had to look a bit up to stare at Joel's eyes. Because of this, Mica had an advantage of acceleration and Joel had an advantage of size. They both came closer. Joel started by kicking his leg on Mica's chest. Mica quickly dodged it, putting all balance on his right foot and chopped on the right side of his rib. Joel stepped 2 steps back. Mica then jumped and spun a kick on Joel's face. Mica's boots had spikes. That's why his face started bleeding from certain points. Joel fell and started touching his bleeding points. Mica tried to finish him, but as he was about to kick him, Joel rolled away. He got up and punched Mica. When Joel punched him, blood spat out of Mica's mouth. " Hey, you know, your father is a great man. He misses you, but not your brother," Mica said. As he said this line, he punched right on Joel's mouth. His 4 teeth fell. Joel's mouth was now a lake of blood. He spat many times but the blood didn't stop. Mica pulled his legs, sat on his chest, and started pounding on him." Trent doesn't love you. He didn't even check on you when I killed your brother's wife and daughter." Joel pushed Mica, got up, and supported himself with the wall. Mica came running and punched him on his pelvis. Mica backed and said," You were left alone at home on the first floor. He just took his daughter and wife to the hospital. He doesn't care about you," Mica whispered in his ear. This time Joel didn't react. He could recall the scenes of that night. He realized that whatever Mica said was unfortunately true. He could see Trent's face on the bullseye of an aiming board. He could hear all of Trent's fake, loving words. He could taste the loveless food Trent made for him. He could feel all of Trent's fake hugs. Mica backed him to the wall, took his knife, and stabbed Joel in his thigh." If I wanted, I could kill you. But your brother would be left alone." Mica said. He took the flare out of Joel's pocket and threw it. Mica climbed the building next to him and sat on the terrace to enjoy the drama.

" Guys, look it's the flare. Joel's in trouble." Scott pointed towards the flare. Trent was confused.' Why does Joel need our help? He is a tough guy. It can't happen. Something's wrong.' Trent thought. Pill quickly took his jeep and started it." C'mon, let's go."

" Should we take Ivan with us?" Trent questioned. Ivan replied," Hey guys, I'm already in the jeep. Let's go."

A few minutes later, they reached the flare. Trent was shocked to see his brother covered in blood. He sat down and lifted Joel's head and put it on his lap. Joel looked straight into Trent's eyes with tears of blood. "Why did you do this brother?" asked Joel stutteringly. " I didn't do nothing," replied Trent quickly. "But you were our best, why did it happen? Please be careful now." Joel took the knife out from his thigh and stuck the knife in Trent's stomach. " He... he... controlled you?" Trent interrogated. Trent fell away. Pill, Scott, and Ivan tried but in vain. They all were stabbed. Joel got up, holding his thigh. He smirked and said, "You never know, who's the rich renegade." Mica came down and patted his back," Welcome to the gang."

Mica took Joel to his sewer. Mica's table was full of documents and photos. The light source was a fire torch. There was a rice straw mat on which Mica slept. There was a constant noise of dripping of water. There was a talkie on a photograph that was circled. Joel picked up the talkie and put it aside. He picked the photo and asked," Isn't that my father? Why is the photo circled?" Mica picked the torch and stared at it," Yes, he is your father, Karen. A great friend of mine. But now that I have become a criminal, he is not my friend anymore." He picked another talkie from his bag and gave it to Joel." Keep it with you. You might need it." Joel turned on the talkie and lay down on the mat, "Mica, why do you kill people? And why did you call me to Angora?" Mica put the torch back and sat on his table," Wait, I'll have to call someone." Mica pushed the rocks beside him. The rocks opened a path to a secret room. Mica came back a few minutes later and said," It was my boss. You know, the person that orders me to kill people. And now he wants me to show you something." Joel missed a beat. The sound of drops of sweat mixed with the sound of dripping of the sewer water. Joel got up with wide eyes and followed Mica to the secret room. Joel could literally smell blood in the room. The floor had blood stains mixed with rust. The room was dark because there was no light in the room. Joel was suffocated in the room. He wanted to leave the room but as Mica torched the fire torch, Joel had changed his mind. There were bodies piled over one another. Joel could hear these bodies screaming for help, but they didn't scream. Joel could see these bodies being killed by Mica, but they were already dead. Mica folded his arms with courage," This is what I have accomplished. Look, we can conquer the whole world if we continue. But those detective friends of yours always ruin my plan. So,

I called all of you to Angora." Joel and Mica went out of the room. Joel again lay down on the mat and asked," Then, why didn't you kill all of us?" Mica laughed," Actually, my boss didn't allow me to do this. So, you can go home now. We'll meet tomorrow. Tomorrow we'll hit big."

Joel quickly left the sewer, took a cab, and went home. On the way, he clicked on his Bluetooth and said," Hey, you guys okay? Did we do well?"

" Excellent, we have succeeded in our plan. We have gained Mica's faith. What did he tell you?" Trent replied.

Joel had fake killed them so that they could succeed. Scott's plan had worked.

" He is a psycho. Whosoever he kills, he keeps them in his secret bunker. There were hundreds of bodies. But the best part is, that he is working for someone."

Scott clenched his fists," I was right that day."

Ivan then asked," Hey Scott, did you realize that you've left drinking."

" No, I didn't. And this ain't time to talk about this."

Joel also said," He also told me that tomorrow, we'll hit big." Trent answered," Don't worry, just be careful. And remember no civilian casualties. Actually, where are you right now?"

" We're in Gingul."

CHAPTER FOUR

Encountered

5 days later

22:00, Warehouse No 4, 2nd floor, Pridety street, Gingul

A woman with a green robe that extended to her knee. She wore pink compression pants and a green woolen cap. She had a small-sized hookah in her mouth. With her was a man in his late 50s, wearing a hat. "Hey guys, it's game over. We've caught you. There's no going back. Come out," said the man. His name was Arthur. The woman beside him was in her 20s and her name was Michelle. Friends called her Shelly. "Hey, you heard that guy. He is a crazy man. Come out, now!" said Shelly. But there was no reply. Shelly took off her coat and said," Now, we'll have to create destruction." Michelle shot the only bullet she had on a machine. The people that were hiding came out of their den," Esta mujer va a pagar," a person said from the group. " You know what, we speak no Spanish but, eso va a doler," said the woman which meant 'that's gonna hurt.' A person took a bat and came to hit Arthur. Arthur ducked, kicked him from his knee, took the bat from his hand, and hit him very hard, enough to break the bat and the person's jaw. All the people ran towards them. Shelly blurted," Hey, I think it's gonna get tough." As they were reaching them, Arthur threw a smoke bomb and disappeared. They tried to find them but in vain. Michelle and Arthur were hiding in a two-compartment almirah. There was a mirror in it. They looked at themselves. Arthur had a black french beard with some whites. His hairs were flicked to the right. He had wrinkles on his temples but was fit as a 20-year guy. Shelly was a young girl from South Korea. She had hair till her neck and bangs from the front. Her hair was blond and her eyes sparkled. Despite her beauty, she was a great detective. Arthur kicked the almirah and jumped onto a person. He chopped on his petto[chest in italian], hit his elbow on his bald head, and let him rest in peace. Michelle too got out of the almirah. She pushed the person behind her and stick him to the wall. She took out her knife and stabbed it just right to the person. " Where is Mica?" she interrogated. The person was confused. Shelly took her empty gun and hit him with it. Arthur took out his phone and called Priter, the boss of the group ' Bangers'.

" Yes, Arthur what news do you have for me?"

" Boss, I and Shelly have killed Mica's sleeper cells."

Priter was perplexed. Priter had a french mustache. He was black. His hairs were white. The combination suited him." Does Mica have sleeper cells?" asked Priter. Arthur blurted out," Yes. This warehouse reads Mica cells." Priter's eyes were red, but he still had a smile. He said," Haven't you heard of Mica's cells? They are selling batteries over there. There are no sleeper cells." Saying this, Priter burst into laughter. Michelle clicked her upper throat with her tongue, showing disapproval," That's a waste of time and energy." Arthur said," Well, I have a great sense of humor. Wanna hear another joke? Now listen. What will you call a train carrying bubblegum?"

" What?" asked Priter widening his eyes with excitement.

" A chew-chew train."

" Man, why aren't you a comedian?" asked Shelly.

" Cause if I would be a comedian, I'll be telling you comedy, not jokes," Arthur said with a little laugh.

" Okay, that was a bad one," Priter said.

H32, Ukina Avenue, Gingul

" Daddy's back," shouted Arthur from his garage. He had a wife and two daughters. One was studying elsewhere and the other was 6 years old. The 6-year-old was named Ava. Ava had worn a blue tunic with no sleeve. She was carrying a small handbag, probably trying to be like her mother. She had a coconut tree ponytail. She came near him and asked, "Pops, You have some jokes for me?" Arthur bent down and started thinking. He took her jute bag, took the air from it, and ate it. He then widened his eyes and said," If I win, then you'll give me some of the chocolate. Deal?"

" Deal," came the reply.

Arthur said," I only know 25 alphabets. I don't know Y."

Ava hit her hand to her forehead," Do I even have to laugh at it? You lost." Arthur held her hand and said,"You know what, I'm a damn cheater. I'll still get it from you."

Ava and Arthur started laughing and cuddling. Suddenly, Arthur broke up and said," You know what Ava, I can't lose you. And one day, I'll make you say that I am the best comedian. I promise you." They both got up and went to the dining table. Their house was beautiful. In the living room, there was a fireplace which made the house warm. Just above that was the television. The room was all white. Around the television and the fireplace were a bunch of artificial plants. The sofas made a U, with the middle sofa facing towards the television. There were many windows around the whole room. And lastly, there was a glass table. " Hey honey, how was your day today?" said Riana, Arthur's wife. She had bangs till her eyes. Her hair reached her shoulder. She was in her 50s too that's why she had some wrinkles. But if there would be a Miss Universe for her age, no one could defeat her. Arthur put some food in his mouth and said," Yeah, it wasn't good. You know, bad decisions. But I am sure, we'll catch Mica. Very soon. Hey kiddo, you won't have your dinner?"

" Pops, I am never late. I finish my things on time," said Ava.

" Okay, let's go. I'll finish my food."

Arthur quickly finished his food and rushed to Ava's room. Her room was purple. Beside her bed was a purple brick design. Arthur climbed the bed and waited for Ava to open her eyes." Hey kiddo, you aren't sleeping, are you?"

" Quit it, daddy. We'll have fun tomorrow. I want to sleep."

" Well, that's my fault. Have a good sleep. Okay, Captain Ava?"

" Okay, Major Papa."

Arthur went down to help his wife with the dishes. When they were finished, they sat down at the table." Arthur, you know how much she loves you. I think we should go on a picnic when you complete this case," suggested Riana. Arthur backed his spine to the chair and said," I know I can't spend time with her and even you. What's the date today?"

" 1 December 2002."

" That's good. Because on New year, I'll finish this case and we'll have lots of fun. Riana, do you know why I am so serious about this case? Because it can be the only chance, I can make my family proud."

Riana patted his shoulder," I know you will."

<u>*08:24, 44th Proximity Street, Bangers Jewel, Gingul*</u>

The room was white. There were many wooden cupboards that had literary books. On the desk was a daruma doll with which Arthur was playing. There was a wooden table with a capacity of 5 chairs." Hey Arthur, Good Morning. Early for the work, eh?" Priter asked. " Not really. I had nothing to do. And this case is big. Where are others?"

" We're here Art."

Bangers had 5 members. Martin, Toy, Levi, Thud, Priter, and Arthur. They all wore black and white coats. They all were in their 20s. Martin had long hairs till his shoulder that were dyed blue, Toy was bald. Levi had 1cm of hair that was dyed blonde. Thud had a red mullet.

They all sat at the table." So, today we will find information about Mica," said Thud. Priter replied," Okay, I and Arthur will go to Sorum's direction. And you all will go in Angora's direction."

They all got out of the building and did as planned.

After walking a few miles, Arthur broke out and said," Hey Prit, Isn't that Joel? The member from 'United'?

" Yes. What are they doing here?"

They both walked toward Joel. As they walked, Joel and Mica pulled them and stick them to the building."Hey, Bangers! Long time no see. You shouldn't be here."

Mica left Priter and said," Joel, let's see what you got." Mica ran fast and disappeared.

Joel backed and said," Okay Bangers. Today, you'll be eliminated from this race. Mica is only ours."

" Huh! You are working for him," Priter said.

" Tsk, you won't understand. Now c'mon, give me some fight."

" Arthur, follow Mica. I'll see him."

CHAPTER FIVE

Race For Mica

" Where is Mica gone now?" Arthur said as he ran, jumping from one roof to the other through the foggy weather. It was 12:00 PM and all the hands of the clock were in the same line.

Medical Emergency Camp, Northside Rijuk, Gingul

" **Trent**, Scott is getting insane again. I had tied him to the bed for treatment and now he doesn't want to stay in bed. Please come back," Pill said with a trembling voice and tensed lower eyelids.

" Pill, you know...can't forsake....sorry.........." Trent's signal was lost." Damnit," Pill said throwing his talkie. The leaves were on the ground because of the fall season. Pill could hear the crunching of leaves from his north. And the next second, Thud was on Pill's chest, pounding on him. Scott somehow got free from the straps. Pill pushed Thud away from his body and got up." Who do we have here? Pill?" asked Thud with evil eyes. Pill took a gun out and shot it, but there were no bullets in it. Thud jumped on him and took a knife out and started pushing it towards Pill's body. Pill held Thud's hand until Scott came out and kicked Thud away from Pill.

Joel was moving around Priter looking straight in his green eyes. Joel took out a knuckle duster from his pocket.

He threw a flare to let his mates know where he is. Priter also took out a nunchaku and stood in position. They could see nothing but their opponents. Priter rotated clockwise and threw the nunchaku at Joel. It wrapped around the hand in which Joel was wearing the knuckle duster. Priter bent his one knee on the ground and threw a boomerang that brought the nunchaku and knuckle duster to Priter. Joel was perplexed. He now had no weapons. Priter ran and hit Joel right on his face. The nunchaku hit Joel's right eye and started bleeding. His eye closed completely. Joel fell down but didn't give up. He rose back, hit Priter with his own nunchaku. Priter fell back and the nunchaku fell from his hand. Joel took advantage and choked Priter with the nunchaku. The choking was so hard that Priter's mouth turned into a river of blood and his eyes turned red. Priter was slowly fading. He hit his head back to Joel's nose. Joel left the nunchaku. Priter quickly got up and hit Joel with the knuckle duster on the same eye he had hit earlier. Joel fell down immediately. Priter also fell down and rolled to the nearby building's corner.

65th street, 45 feet from the flare, Gingul

" **Did Joel** tell anything?" asked Ivan.

Trent replied," Yeah. He was saying he saw Priter, from the bangers."

As they kept on walking and talking, Martin, Toy and Levi jumped on both of them." Hey Trent, how you doing?"

Ivan kicked Levi from himself and pulled Martin away from Trent. Trent took a compass out from his pocket and hit Toy on his nose. Toy rolled away, fluttering from pain. Martin took his gun out and aimed at Ivan. Ivan ran, slid and pulled Martin's legs. Martin fell down and his gun slid away into the drain. Levi punched Trent but he blocked it. Levi then stepped on Trent's thigh and jumped to the other side and choked Trent. Ivan sat on Martin's chest, hit him with his elbow and ran to save Trent. But Trent was already free from the choke. Trent took out his knife to finish him but saw Mica on the rooftop of a building. He threw away his knife and gave Toy a hand." Don't worry. Our doctor will fix it. C'mon, we all want Mica," Trent said. Toy got up and said," Yes. Together we can defeat him. C'mon Martin and Levi, let's go."

" **Hey Priter, do you copy**? I saw Mica coming towards you. Please, we should unite now," Arthur said.

Scott took out a knife and started stabbing it. Thud held his hand. " Scott, don't do it. We are a team now. Track Joel's place and reach there fast," Trent said on the talkie. Scott rolled away and said," Hey calm down now. I don't know why but we are a team."

Thud spat blood and said," Oh thank god! I was gonna die right there."

CHAPTER SIX

Federated

" Hey Joel, you okay?" asked Pill bending down towards him. Pill gave Priter and Joel a syringe. " Okay, so United and Bangers are now federated. Let's go and catch that scoundrel," Trent declared.

" I have to take Scott, Joel, Toy, and Priter with me. They are critical," Pill said.

They all started following the trail Mica had left. They crossed many Trullo houses fighting through the dusk until Mica came and stood in front of them." Oh! Please leave me. I won't do it again. You wanted me to say that huh?" Mica said widening his lips and raising his eyebrows. Arthur blurted out," Course not. How 'bout that?"

Mica clicked on his goggles and it read 'Cabron'. Mica raised his hand. And the next moment, there were many people dressed as Mica. Trent's group's every single person had to fight with a Mica. " I will fight, You!" The 'real' Mica said pointing towards Arthur. Arthur came forward and said," Well you know what, I don't speak Spanish but elegiste a la persona equivocada,"[You chose the wrong person] Arthur said and took a wakizashi[small katana] out. Mica wore a shin guard on his both arms which had a pointed end. Mica ran and jumped with his hand pulled back, ready to strike. Arthur dodged, putting all his balance on his left leg, and tried to stab the waki. Mica blocked it with his shin and pushed Arthur back. Mica then stabbed Arthur with the pointed end. It was small, that's why Arthur wasn't injured that much but it still was paining. Arthur rolled Mica to the right side and started stabbing it. Mica blocked it with both his hand. As the waki was just about to enter his body, he rolled away and punched Arthur in the face. Arthur lied supine and pulled the blade away from the base. The base had another but a small blade. Arthur threw the small blade on Mica's thigh. Mica gave a small groan and took the blade out. Mica clicked on his shin. The shin opened and Mica fixed the blade in front of it. Mica was walking putting all his weight on his right leg as his left leg was injured. Arthur got up and wiped blood dripping through his mouth.

Trent choked the Mica he was facing. He pushed Trent away. Trent supported himself with the building. He quickly took out a blade and went to stab Trent. Trent held his hand for a few seconds then turned clockwise. The blade stuck in the building. Trent took advantage and pushed the fake Mica through it. Trent took the bloody blade out of his chest and went on to save his mates.

Ivan was down. The fake Mica was standing above him. Ivan kicked him very hard. He backed a bit and took his knife to kill Ivan. But as he took the knife, he was shot in the head by Thud. As the fake Mica was falling, Ivan took a screwdriver out from his back pocket and put it under the place fake Mica was falling. Mica's flesh was torn apart because of the screwdriver." You have a great gun," Thud said. Ivan took his gun back and said," Yeah, this gun is used from my grandfather's era."

Martin was fighting two Micas at the same time. He took out his batons and hit them hard. He finished the fight by hitting the batons on both ears of a Mica at the same time.

Trent opened his pocket and took his talkie out," Is everyone okay? The real Mica is fighting with Arthur. We are pretty far from them. Let's get there quickly.

Mica was battering Arthur with his shins. The shins were turning red. Arthur somehow held his waki in his hand and stabbed it in Mica's stomach. Mica left grip of his shins. He was crying from pain. His feet were sweeping the ground. He couldn't take the waki out of his stomach so he gathered all his power and broke it with one end still inside his stomach. He put a hand on his stomach and got up. Arthur was now thinking,' What will it take?'. And he was suddenly reminded by his brain,' But the stakes are high. And his death is a necessity.' Arthur got up and clicked his Bluetooth. He took the shins Mica had dropped. Mica came running with the broken waki. Arthur blocked it with his shins. Mica took the advantage and took out a pocket knife and stabbed it in Arthur's right portion of the chest. Arthur groaned but didn't fall. He bent down with one shin defending himself from the blade and hit Mica on the same spot where he had been already stabbed. Mica turned, lifted Arthur from the back, and slammed him to the ground lying on his stomach. Because of the impact to the ground, the pocket knife went in and tore Arthur's shoulder completely. Arthur's pain was limitless. But he didn't make a noise. Instead, Mica took the blade and as he was about to end Arthur, Michelle jumped in and kicked Mica away." Oh, Art, you're severe." Shelly spun a kick on Mica. Mica fell on his stomach. Shelly took his katana, swung it, and finished Mica in style. Arthur got up and reached Mica with widened eyes." Did we just do it? Shelly, we've done what none has done in a year," Arthur cried. " Well, you know. Women aren't less," Shelly said.

Trent and company reached the spot and threw their weapons. But Trent was still concerned. He took a syringe out from his pocket and stuck it in Mica's heart. " That's gonna wake him up just for a minute. And then, he'll again die," Trent said. He took a portable tape recorder and turned it on. Mica woke up with jerks. Trent held his ears and said," How do you feel now? Why did you kill so many people?" Mica stuttered and said," I..I won't tell you." Trent's eyes tensed up. He backed from him and sat on the ground."What happened, Trent?" Arthur asked putting his hand on Trent's knee. Trent's eyes were filled up. He swallowed his saliva with difficulty and said," He is not the Mica that killed my family. His voice is deep. The Mica that killed my family had a light voice." He took the recorder to Joel and asked," Is he the Mica that you were working with?" Joel listened to it 2 to 4 times and said," No, it isn't."

" Then who the heck is the real Mica?" Toy asked from the bed he was lying on.

Trent said," Nobody knows. Scott, can I talk with you for some time alone?"

They both went to the other camp." Okay, let me tell you something. Gingul was my birthplace. And it is the place where my family was murdered. And I don't know why but I see my daughter in you. You are a smart guy. You are a skilled guy. That's why I want you to take all of us, United and Bangers, forward and provide us that killer. So, you are the headquarters and lead us wherever you want. I've tried my best but I couldn't do anything. I believe in you."

Scott took a sip from his beer bottle and said," Thank you and I surely won't fail you."

Trent hugged him and said," But remember I ain't retiring."

Scott laughed and said," Of course, father."
Trent laughed and said," That's my son."

CHAPTER SEVEN

New Captain:New Beginning

<u>*4:58 AM, Medical Emergency Camp, Northside Rijuk, Gingul*</u>

" Hey guys, our eyes our puffed up. Okay, I understand it's important to get Mica. But we should have some sleep," Scott said with his eyes almost closed. There were nimbus clouds. The falling of rain on the stones made a beautiful sound. The petrichor was up in the air and a light breeze was going on. The moon was still there but the daylight had already come out. Joel got up from his bed with his one eye still covered. He pushed Scott to the wall from his collar," What do you think that whatever you say we'll follow? We all want that guy. I don't wanna just stay here." Joel left him and flipped his stretcher. Trent held him and said," Hermano, calm down. We'll get to him." Joel started laughing and said," Well you know what Trent, I should have killed all of you." Joel said and stabbed Trent. Trent vomited some blood and fell. Everyone else pulled Joel away from Trent. Pill said," Keep him away. Or Trent would die." Joel kicked Pill away from Trent. Ivan picked up his gun and aimed at Joel. Joel took his gun and hit him in the face. Pill took Trent with him somewhere else for treatment. Scott kicked on Joel's face and said," Please stop!

Try to understand." Joel lifted Scott and threw him and then said," I don't need advice from a man that gets crazy every 15 minutes." Martin, Levi, and Thud tried but in vain. Joel banged his hand on the table and said," I am crazy." Joel felt a touch on his mouth." Shhhh, don't. It's me, Mica. I knew you would betray. And now you injured these guys. Why?" Mica's voice was of a Russian accent. Scott pulled Mica's legs. Martin and Thud held his hands. Joel hit Mica in the face with a baton. Joel looked at the baton and said," Hey Martin, you've got some good batons." Trent and Pill came inside. Scott got up and came face to face with Mica. Trent said," Hey guys, how was my acting? Did I vomit the ketchup well?" Trent said this in a scoffing tone. Scott bent down staring at Mica's goggles. Trent took out a transmitter from his pocket," These are yours, aren't these?" Joel came forward and hit him again with the batons. Mica heard something from his Bluetooth and said," Okay, I'll tell you. Why I kill. Have you ever wondered why some houses have at least one member alive? Because they follow my path. And they'll get salvation. You kill and eat. I kill and feed. Humans don't understand. I feed those people to the animals. The guys that I left were vegans. You all kill those animals for their meat. I kill people for their meat."

Trent was taken aback. He said," Mica, why do you have this feeling?"

Mica grinned, " Our story is long. We must unfold it slowly. And if you continue to interfere, I must kill you too."

Scott stood up," What do you mean by 'ours'?

Mica took a taser out from his pocket," That's enough for today." Mica shot Levi and ran as fast as he could.

Nobody followed him. Everyone's eyes were adrift. Scott's sweat dropped to the ground and mixed with the sound of rain. Toy said," Now what? It's a dead end. We can't do anything." Arthur took the shins he had got from Mica during the fight," Hey Scott, I have a plan. Are we ready?" Scott's eyes entangled and he fell to the ground with a thump.

5:30 AM, Medical Hospital, Sorum

The hospital was destructed. The lights were fluttering. The doctors were killed in their surgical suits. There were three beds in the hospital room. The people were suffocated to death, except one who was still alive. With a knife stabbed to his chest, Scott was still alive in the room.

Trent was in his apartment in Sorum, looking out from his window. The moon was out. He was pleased to see those bars and stars after a long time. He took his phone called the doctor." What has happened? Why isn't he picking the call? Ah damn it, I'll go and see myself." Trent sat in his jeep and went to the hospital. The roads were slippery because of the continuous rain. The music could be heard from the bars as Trent passed by them. Trent reached. The hospital was a small building with a single floor. The lights were off. Trent got out of his car and said," No, something's wrong." Trent rushed inside. His swallowing became difficult as he saw everybody killed. He went inside the room where Scott was breathing heavily. Trent rushed to Scott's bed and sat down. Scott looked at Trent with his neck lifted and said," Father, I don't know what has happened. Please, I don't want to die." Scott's heart rate was decreasing on the monitor. **Trent wore his gloves and carefully took the knife out of Scott's chest.** " Pill, immediate help. Medical hospital, Sorum. Please!" The knife read Strumy which was 15km away from Sorum. Trent took the knife and put it inside his pocket. Trent held Scott's hand and thought," Why do these things happen with Scott? Does Mica hate him badly? And why does Mica keep telling us where he is?

Scott gets insane, he falls to the ground. We brought him to Sorum and this happened. There is something wrong."

The hospital door banged and Pill came inside." Oh no, Scott are you okay?" Pill pressured on his wound. "Trent, we'll have to take him to the nearest hospital. It's small. It's in Angora. We gotta take him there."

The car was then occupied and they left for Angora. On the way, Trent asked," Hey Pill, can you tell why he acts insane?"

" I was trying to but was not able to. We'll have to take him to a big hospital. In Strumy, for instance. You should call Joel, Ivan, and Bangers and tell them to reach Angora, pronto."

6th of December, 2002, Angora

" It's been two days. I've been just wasting my life on this rusted iron bed. I want to solve the case, man. You tell me that Mica keeps injuring me. Why?" Scott said with Pill beside him." Man, I know you gotta know. But this is getting difficult. Mica keeps us engaged, keeps us telling where he is and then he vanishes. We try to fight him, he wins and vanishes." Pill replied sipping a bottle of beer. Scott pulled the bottle away from Pill and said," That's for me, dumpy. And you know, it reminds me of my family. My family steals, tortures then vanishes. I'm relatable."

" So, Scott, are you ready to rock again?" Joel came in and asked.

" Let's go. Let's get to Strumy."

Strumy Unifori, Strumy

Strumy was situated in the middle of mountains. It had some shops and houses in a chain, a gas station for travelers but it had run out of gas. The road was stone-paved. And just a few meters ahead was an unorthodox sewer pipe with an opening sticking out from the road. The sun was finally out." Well, it'll be easy to find Mica cause this village is small." Ivan said with widened and pleasing eyes. As Scott had entered the village, he was hooked to the sewer pipe. " So boss, where are we headed?" Trent asked with a little smile on his face as he knew Scott was hooked and interested in the sewer pipe. "Wow, this place reminds me of a joke. Haven't cracked in years. Okay, listen, what does a monkey do when it's hungry?"

Ivan and Pill started thinking deeply. At last, they gave up and asked," What is it?"

"Stop it, you're gonna die laughing."

Ivan replied," Okay, we aren't listening."

Scott said," Hey wait, I'm telling. When a monkey is hungry, it eats something."

The place was quiet and the only thing that could be heard was the breeze." I'm sorry. That was a bad one," Scott said lowering his head. Arthur came and patted on his shoulder," Man, my daughter says the same thing."

" Hey comedians, can we now move on somewhere?" Priter said. "Where your guns at big guys?" Trent asked pointing towards Martin and Levi." **We left them. The ammo was limited and we know that Mica doesn't want us killed. He wants something else,**" Levi replied." Okay, so there is that unorthodox pipe over there. And we should start from there. Cause Joel told us that he lives in sewers," Scott said. "Well, then he loves pigs too. Do you know my mama gave me small piggy candies? We should get some for him too," Toy said showing some pain in between because of the injury in his eye. Trent noticed it and said, "Man, I'm sorry for that injury." They went to the sewer pipe. Then, at first, Scott stepped on it and coiled himself so that the ride could be butter smooth, and then everyone else followed. The sewer pipe ended up in an underground cave that was lit up with purple fire torches. There was a throne with infinite pointed ends. And the person sitting on it was Mica." Hey, knew you would be here. Love sewers, huh?" Trent said with a confident voice that echoed around the cave. Mica got up from his throne and came forward with his hands floating." Well Trent, would you please go and rub the wall beside you?" Trent slowly went to the wall and rubbed it gently. A brick fell and beside it was a plate with the name Karen Grunt on it." Oh shit, it's my father. This cave was made by my father. There were riots all over Gingul and my father had invented something extraordinary. He hid it and left this place. And now, as far as I know, he's dead. And he told me that this cave is huge. But sadly, I don't know any of the codes he used and I don't know what are the traps here. It's all by ourselves." "Don't worry man, we don't need to solve it. Today we'll kill Mica," Scott said looking at Mica with evil eyes. Mica took a katana out from his scabbard and touched it with his lips." Oh really," Mica said and flicked his sword towards the Bangers and United. Footsteps could be heard. People with bandanas on their mouth came with guns." I don't like guns. You do this work with two people having a gun on each person's head," Mica said putting his sword back." How will it benefit you and us?" Joel asked." How it will benefit us is not your business. But if you do it, I am ready for a final fight with you."

" What if you are lying?" Scott asked, fluttering his hands as he was starting to get insane.

Mica smirked and said," Have I ever?"

" But," Trent asked. " Shhhh!" Mica replied.

" Hey, you, you know what, kids go to pee from that sound. And I am dry from the inside," Scott said and fell to the ground. Mica quickly ran to Scott and stabbed an injection on his neck." What are you doing?" Arthur asked." I don't need weak people here. Guards, take him away from my eyes before I say something. I have to take these guys to mini hell, to the game of the unsure,"replied Mica.

CHAPTER EIGHT

Game Of The Unsure: Peril Ahead

The big door had opened. The door had spikes attached with a little part available for pushing. The groups went in. The lights had changed color. The fire torches were now red. Mica was gone. And the groups were taken hostage by the people in bandanas and guns. The way was diverging in 5 different ways. The ground started shaking and digging sounds could be heard." Work, it's just a bulldozer," a person from the bandana group said who was in charge of Levi. The two groups divided themselves into groups of 2. " Guys, but who's the new leader?" Arthur asked. Trent laughed silently," How 'bout you?" Arthur smirked and said," Huh, I knew I was the chosen one. But now I got a load of burden." " So you don't wanna be the leader?" Martin asked. " Shut up, I was just kidding," came the reply.

The groups were divided into Martin and Joel, Arthur and Ivan, Toy and Trent, Thud and Pill, and Priter and Levi. As Bangers were more experienced than United, that's why they all put themselves in a mixer and mixed themselves with their 'old enemy' group that now had become friends. Martin and Joel stood at the first way. They all placed them in front of ways 2,3,4 and 5 respectively.

Martin and Joel went into the circle opening. As they kept walking forward, the way turned into a small bridge with sewer water beneath. The road was blocked. They jumped to the sewer water and flowed with the current. The water at the end struck a wall. They climbed out and kept walking. " So Joel, why were you working with Mica?" Martin asked. Joel looked at him and said," Do you know what a renegade is?" " No," came the reply. " Then just remember that it never happened," Joel said. " I don't think I got my answer but I won't fight a person who is 2 times larger than me and has had a great match with my boss who is a black belt in judo," Martin answered. Joel giggled and said," Yes, keep it that way." Hey, I just noticed that we're free. The people are not here," Martin said with widened eyes. " Hey chipmunk, said anything about us?" The person in bandana said from above." C'mon, follow us through this ladder. The way is up here. And a puzzle is waiting for you. They climbed the ladder and saw a big door with a place where there were numbers and letters written. The wall read' -:'-=;<> '. " Wow, now how do we solve it? Han, Bandana guys?" Martin asked. Bandana people turned and whispered to each other," Yep, he is a chipmunk!" Martin replied," Hey, I think that's not whispering. I know you said chipmunk. Now what, should I chuck like him?" Joel stepped backward and whispered to himself," Blockheads!" He came forward and said," Okay enough, we'll need Scott for this." Bandana people aimed their guns at both of them and said," Oh! Now we have orders that if you take his name, you're dead. 3....2....1." Scott came with a knife and stabbed a person from the bandana people. The other person turned around. Martin jumped on him and Joel finished him with a foot on his head. " Man, that was some good entry," Joel said hugging his buddy. Scott replied,"

You know, killed the person in charge of me and took a knife. I saw that Mica was not here so I came running to the first tunnel. Who is in charge?" " Arthur, but he is a good guy and funny too," Martin said. " So, Scott here we have a big problem, can you solve it?" Joel questioned. " Hm, this sentence here is written in Noik code, the hardest language to learn. And I am sorry I haven't studied it. Don't know how your father studied it," Scott replied. " So now what?" Martin asked. " Joel, is your father still alive? Or are his books still at your house? Cause we'll need the Noik code," Scott said. Joel didn't say anything and quickly rushed back to his apartment. The apartment was wooden floored and was congested with objects. And Joel loved to live in it. There was a separate room with a glass sliding door that had potted flowers. Joel rushed to his library and separated his father's books. As he was separating them, he remembered that his father was a friend of Mica. And it could be possible that he would still be alive. He thought why his father had left codes in the cave. He knew his father was a doctor and was very rich. Scott said on the earpiece," Hey Joel, found anything?" Joel woke up and said," Yes, I, uh, found the Noik codebook." As he said these lines, his door opened with a person standing. It was Mica." So, you followed me till here?" Joel broke his earpiece and threw it away. Mica was standing with a baseball bat. Joel stood with his fists clenched as he was 2 times larger than Mica. But he had already faced him and it was very tough to defeat Mica.

Back at the cave, Scott had turned insane again. He fell on Martin's shoulder. Martin lifted him and said," Hey bud, you okay?" Scott pushed him back and jumped on his chest. He headbutted Martin many times. Martin's eyes rolled and he pushed Scott away from him. Martin grabbed the gun and shot Scott in the leg. But Scott didn't fall. Martin again shot him and this time the bullet penetrated his thigh. Scott fell to the ground. Martin punched him one time and Scott fainted. Martin rolled away and contacted Trent and Arthur on his earpiece and said," Hey guys, Scott had escaped the prison and had come to help us. Joel is at his house fighting with Mica. And Scott had turned insane again. So I shot him in the legs. Trent, send Pill over here. And Art you go to Joel's house and save him from Mica. Take my car if you want." Arthur said to himself," I shouldn't have brought this chipmunk with me."

CHAPTER NINE

Game Of The Unsure: Fierce Attacks On 7th

7th of December

The night had passed and they were still in it

Priter and Levi had injured the bandana people. They came across a place with a slot in it. Below it was lava. They went forward to the wall and the wall read something that was not visible. The wall smelled of blood. " Hey Lev, I think we have to make red color here. Magenta and yellow. We mix them and we can see what's written. They went back to the hall and picked a fire torch from there. As they were walking back towards the place, a bandana guy, that was injured by them held Levi's foot. Levi said," Go Prit, I'll take care of these guys. And yes, take this lipstick for the magenta color. I don't know why I have it." Levi kicked him with his left foot. The bandana guy slid his head away and pulled Levi down. Levi rolled and hit his head with his knee. The bandana guy rebounded and headbutted Levi to the wall. Levi's eyes rolled and his head was covered with blood. He reversed and took small rebar that was lying on the ground and stabbed the guy in the stomach. The guy vomited blood on Levi's back. Levi fell and touched his head. The guy also fell and died. Levi was laughing until the other bandana guy punched him in the face. The guy was furious and took out the rebar from his mates' stomach. The clicking sound could be heard when the mass was rubbed against steel. The guy took it and came to hit Levi. Levi got up and stabbed a nail in his eye. The bandana guy's eye was continuously flowing from blood. Levi was caught by the neck and the guy started choking him. The guy took out polythene and covered Levi's face with it. " Bye," he said and stabbed Levi in the head by the rebar. Priter ran towards the guy and shot him with his gun. Priter sat beside Levi and collected the blood that was leaking in a test tube. He wrote' Third time I've had depression and pasted it on the test tube and put it back inside his pocket. He clicked on his earpiece and said," Guys, Levi has left us forever." Priter went back to the room and decoded the code. The code read' Ravenous for souls'. Priter took no time and understood what the code said. He clicked his earpiece and said," Bye guys, I gotta go meet Levi." The slot was wide enough and Priter jumped in it. The lava disappeared and there was a trampoline. He got back to the top and said," Well, that was unexpected." He again clicked his earpiece and said," Sorry guys, wrong news, Priter ain't going nowhere." A door opened but it had nothing but cement." Well, I was unlucky, there was nothing here. Let's go and meet other guys.

Pill was with Martin, treating Scott. He took his forceps and pulled out the bullet." It's not a normal bullet. It's a tracer. It contains Anaphylaxis. But it is mild.," Pill said. " I should take this gun with me," Martin said with a proud voice. " This gun is not for chipmunks," Pill said with a giggle. He took out adrenaline and injected it through his thigh." He'll be up in a second," Pill said. Scott woke up with a jerk and said," Man, I gotta know why I get insane. And what happens when I'm insane." Pill stood up and said," I'm afraid bud but I think it's Schizophrenia or Autism. We'll have to go to the big hospital in Strumy, with extra protection." Scott took the gun and asked," Joel not here yet?"

" He's stuck in a fight with Mica," Martin answered." So we gotta roll. Let's go," Scott declared.

Joel had punched Mica a few times but still, Mica had the upper hand. Mica ran and flipped over his head. He grabbed Joel's back and hit it with his knees. Joel grunted and caught him by his throat and sent him flying out of the window. The house was just 1 floor tall but still, the damage was enough to keep Mica down. They both were now on the burning road. Mica got up but fell a few times trying. Joel reached him and punched him with all his strength. The punch was strong and Mica spat blood. " Remember the last time we fought? You were here, where I am right now. You left me but I won't let you go," Joel said. Mica replied," Really, my friend? Always, the hero gets wrecked and then reverses the situation. Watch me give an example." Mica kicked him back, spun a kick on his face, and grabbed him by the throat. Joel's eyes were turning red and he was slowly fainting. Mica was almost going to kill Joel but Arthur arrived at the scene." Hey you know you are a non-compos mentis? Now back off or I'll..I'll, damn I can't kill you. But I'll try. And you know what when you'll be fighting me you're..you're, I'll piss my pants," Arthur said. Joel replied in an angry voice," Man! What're you doing?" Arthur replied," Hey you know, I'll make him laugh, and then I'll suddenly attack him." " Really cabron?" Arthur took out his shins and put them on his hands." These are yours, aren't they?" Arthur asked Mica. Mica ran and kicked Arthur. Arthur blocked it and hit Mica with the shins. Mica backed up and ran around Arthur at full speed and suddenly attacked Arthur. He grabbed Arthur's head and tried to spin it and end his game. But Scott, Pill, and Martin arrived. Mica left him and ran away. " Guys did need help. Thanks!" Arthur said chuckling." Hey, I just noticed he is afraid when we're together. So next time, we'll catch him surely," Scott said. Scott tied himself in the car because he knew he was gonna turn insane again. Pill hugged Scott and said," Good boy!" Joel asked Martin," Do you know where Trent is?"

CHAPTER TEN

Game Of The Unsure: One Way Up

Trent and Toy were going on. Their way seemed endless. They turned back halfway and reached the hall. It was one day and they were hungry and thirsty. The teams were reunited and they decided to go back to their apartments. The sun was out and was striking Scott's tired and sweaty face." Guys, let's go to my apartment. It'll be nice if we stay together. Cause we don't know when Mica might strike us," Trent said.

They sat at a table with a beer in their hands." It has become ridiculous. Scott, you know we can't keep just following everything he says. We need to do something quickly. Either we follow that killer's way or we create our plans," Ivan said. " That's not how it works, Ivan! You don't want to lose your friends 'cause you've already lost your damn family!" Scott said, banging his hand on the table." I'm sorry, I didn't mean to hurt you," Scott said in a low voice. " Yeah, yeah, it's okay. I just loved my family and I wanted to get revenge," Ivan replied.

Ivan continued," Had a good father. Had a good mother, both loved me till the end. And a younger sister, who died before I had seen her. I had a good father, but my father didn't have a good father. My father was stuck in traffic. My father's father, because I didn't like him that's why I didn't call him grandpa, took my mom to the hospital in Sorum. I was sleeping at home. And when it turned out that I had a sister, he was not happy. He sat in his car, kicked my mother out, and drove his car away. My father found my mother and took her back home. He might have killed my sister till now." Trent bumped his head up and down and said," Man, it must have been tough. You're 23 and it's been 4 years till your family died." Ivan's tears rolled down his cheeks," You guys are my family. And whatever you say, you'll say for my good." Scott kept his hand on Ivan's shoulder and said," Don't let us down."

" It's time to go Scott. Let's fix your problem," Pill said.

Scott and Pill got in the jeep. It was daytime and they were sure that Mica would attack. So they took guns with them. But this time Mica stayed shut. He didn't appear. Scott had reached the hospital with Pill and was admitted to a room. The doctor came out after an hour and said," Dr. Pill, it will take some time for diagnosis. At least it's not possible to know what he is suffering from today." Pill replied," No, we can't afford it. We need him. Any other options?" The doctor sat down with arms on his thigh and said," Then Dr. Pill, you'll have to stay with us for a few days and tell us everything that happens with Scott." Pill didn't think much and said," Deal." Scott was released. Scott alone got in the jeep and went back where everyone was waiting and discussing. Trent took out his earpiece and contacted Pill," Where are you, Pill? We need you too. Who'll be our doctor?" Pill replied," I'm sorry. And please don't take seriously whatever I say. But your father had taught you everything about medicine in front of me. You and I are of the same level. But you denied being a doctor because you thought it was useless. Doctors are the saviors of the world." Trent ended the call and put his forehead on his hands. His fingers formed a triangle that covered his nose. He closed his eyes. Joel kept his hand on Trent's shoulder and started massaging it." Our father had always loved you more than me. Because you brought laurels when you were in school and college. You made our family proud. You made United proud. But you didn't love your father. Whatever he taught you, you denied to follow or remember it. Even though you were the adopted child, you were treated as a part of the family," Joel said with his eyes filled with big tears. Trent suddenly turned his head up because he heard a loud bang. He saw that Scott had lifted Toy and had slammed him on the table. Joel caught Scott and said," Calm down, buddy. Trent, Scott is turning insane. Do something!" Arthur reached Scott and massaged his head," Calm down, sleep. Sleep," Scott's eyes were adrift and he was falling asleep until Mica came inside and kicked Arthur away. Arthur got up and said," Trent and Joel, take Scott somewhere else safe. Ivan, I, and other members will take care of him. Run! Trust me!" Trent gave Scott GHB and made him faint. They left. Mica took a taser out and said," Why did you leave the work I had given you? But thank you, Priter. The cemented door you opened for me has done our work. Now as promised, I provide you address for the final fight. No running back. But I think only six of you are going to fight me. Because I want to kill all of those who left this place right now. So give me the way and make this easy. Or I'll have to make it hard." " Well,'cabron', I've learned some of the words you said to me. But, simply, we ain't gonna let you reach them," Arthur said taking out shins that he had got from Mica in the previous fight in Gingul. Mica shot Martin in the leg. Martin fell and said,"

Why Man, this is hurting." Mica replied," This ain't gonna kill you, chipmunk. I don't wanna kill you all." Arthur ran and slid onto the ground. Mica kicked Arthur. Arthur fell and quickly got up. He punched Mica on his stomach. Mica bent down. Arthur sat down and hit Mica with the shins. Mica turned and spat blood. Thud hit his knee onto Mica's head. Mica's nose started bleeding. Toy kicked Mica in the abdomen. Priter held Mica's hands and smashed him to the wall.

Bureau Of Investigation In Sorum

" Yes Sir, we're trying. We're trying our best," A person in a black suit said. The person went up to the office and said," Boss, people are rushing from the door. And we haven't found Mica yet. Bangers and United are not able to do it. We should do something, Pritla ma'am." The whole building was in charge of all the groups and detectives out there in Sorum. Bangers and United were one of them. Pritla was incharge." Well, then, fire them. Bangers and United are fired. Seize their properties, their cars, everything they own. They didn't do what we expected. They deserve it," Pritla said. The person replied," But ma'am, none has found Mica yet. So, we shouldn't discriminate against them." " Shut up. Do as I say. Send the cavalry," came the reply. Bulldozers were sent." What is your problem?" Riana said, hugging her daughter, Ava. People are cruel. They were too. They didn't see. The people who were talking held Riana's hand." Leave my mom. My father will scold you," Ava said. Riana stood still. When the people saw it, they started kicking them both. They threw them out of the house. Riana took her phone, and called Arthur. Arthur's phone was busy. Riana and Ava kept pushing the people to let them into the house. The person in charge called Pritla," Boss, they are not letting us.

What should we do?" Pritla laughed and said," Kill them!" The person too laughed and said," Hey Riana, come." Riana ran to him and said," You shouldn't be doing it."

Sin People

Arthur punched Mica many times. Mica headbutted Arthur. Martin was finally free. He crawled to the taser and aimed at Mica. He shot the taser. Arthur came in between and was shot by the taser." What're you doing, Art? I was shooting Mica," Martin said. Mica took advantage and kicked Priter away and pulled out another taser from his pocket and shot everyone." Adios, I am ready for a fight in Strumy.," Mica said and left. Martin said," How does he know where they have left for?"

Riana and Ava were sitting in a room. The in-charge came inside and said," Don't worry. It's not your fault. It's your husband's fault. A stout person also came inside with two cleavers. Riana was still sobbing. But Ava kept strong." Why is he here?" Ava asked. The in-charge laughed and said," He just here to cut meat." The room was like a prison with no windows but the door. Riana and Ava were sitting on a chair. Ava had written something on a paper which she had kept in her pocket. The incharge left the room and said," Butcher, today we need good meat."

" **Scott's gonna wake up in 5 minutes. We should take him somewhere safe,**" Trent said, as Joel was driving the car. Joel looked from the rear mirror and said," Our friends couldn't stop him. He's chasing us." Joel's car's speedometer suddenly started decreasing. And it stopped." What happened Joel?" Trent asked. Joel replied," Let's run. The car's out of fuel." They got out of the car. Joel kept Scott on his back. They ran to the nearby alley. Mica came forward and said," Trying to get away from me?" Joel put Scott on the ground and said," Don't remember last time huh?" Mica came running to Joel and flipped over Joel's head. Joel caught him in mid-air and threw him to the ground. He took his legs and lifted him. Then, he slammed Mica into the nearby building. Mica's nose broke and started bleeding heavily. Mica got up and raised his finger. Again, many Mica came. Joel lifted Scott back up and ran back to the apartment.

" **Thank you, doctor, see you tomorrow,**" The doctor said waving his hand to Pill. Pill was in his car and drove back to the apartment. As he was driving, he saw a loud crowd gathering at a place. His phone was ringing. It was Pritla." Dr. Pill, your group and Bangers' apartments are taken back. You all are fired." Pill grunted and threw his phone away. But he wasn't much angry, because he was attracted to the crowd. He got out of his car. He pushed everyone away, saying,' I am a doctor. He went to the front. The house's plate read,' Arthur, Ava, and Riana'. Two wooden chairs were laid down. And on it was Ava and Riana. The chairs were red. Riana's head was chopped off her body and was lying on her legs. They both were tied to chairs. Near the chairs was a cleaver knife full of blood. Pill closed his eyes. The rain had started again. Big and hard drops stroke Pill's face. Pill's tears were mixed with the rain. He took another phone out of his pocket and called Arthur. Arthur was finally free from the stun. Pill's voice was stuttering. His throat was heavy." Hey, Arthur, uh, please. Come fast to your house. Tell, tell everybody, we are, are fired." Arthur's eyebrows raised and he quickly ran to his jeep and drove to his house.

" **Trent, we are at the apartment,**" Joel said, exhaling deeply. Scott was up." Scott, you are a pain for us, you know that? C'mon, let's walk fast," Trent said. The room was all silent. The table was occupied with sad faces." Guys, what happened?" Scott asked. Martin replied," We couldn't do it. We all are fired. Our apartments have been taken back. Arthur has his family. Glad, we don't have a family." Trent crossed his eyebrows and asked," Where is Arthur?"

Arthur was at his home. The crowd was now gone. The blood was dried up. Pill's eyes were still wet. Arthur sat down beside Riana with no expression. Arthur kept his hand on Ava's bloody thigh and felt something in her pocket. He put his hand inside Ava's pocket and found a paper rolled many times. The paper read,' Hey Papa, a butcher is here and he is very nice. Today we are gonna eat nice meat. I hope you come early and eat with us.' The paper had space and again read,' Father, a person wearing a black mask and black clothes killed my mother. He also hit me with a knife. Come fast, please. Or I am going to die.' Arthur could hear Ava's voice while reading it. Arthur had no expression. He got up and sped off with his jeep to Strumy.

" **Where is Arthur, Pill?**" Trent asked. Pill replied in a low voice," He's probably out to kill Mica. Because he is the one who killed his family." Everyone was there. The paper they read made their eyes red.

Mica was in the same old sewer cave. He had two daggers and was waiting for anyone to show up. If he would have wanted, he would have kept a gun with him. Nonetheless, he was a true man. Arthur knew it and had brought the shins that he had 'borrowed' from Mica. Arthur came with still no expression and said," You killed my family?" " Yes," came the reply. Then, there was no talk. It was just calm before the storm. The weapons were lifted. And disaster was ready to happen. The fight would contain a flood. Flood of blood. And fortunately, it did.

CHAPTER TWELVE

Once In A Lifetime

Mica was down on the ground with his nose bleeding. Arthur had no expression but Mica could sense anger in Arthur's eyes. Arthur's shins were blunt. Mica's daggers were new. " Your shins are great," Arthur said, removing a shin and stabbing it on Mica.

Scott was at the apartment. He was sleeping. His eyes opened suddenly because of a bang at his door. Scott was not in the mood of fighting. He blocked the door with a shelf so that the person couldn't break into the house. He called Trent and said," Trent, someone's breaking into the apartment. And I am tired. I checked from the window. It's not Mica. It's an old man." Trent replied," I don't think he's hostile. But if he does anything, hold him off. I'll send Pill right away."

It was nighttime. And this time Mica was on top of Arthur. He was trying to stab Arthur in the neck. Arthur had blocked from his arm. The dagger touched Arthur's neck. Arthur's neck was bleeding. Arthur pushed Mica away. And threw his only shin on Mica. The shin got stuck in Mica's nose." I don't need shins," Arthur said. Mica replied," You wanna check what my daggers can do?" Arthur replied," You killed my family. I didn't even get time to bury them." This time Arthur dropped his first tear after the incident. His eyes had turned red. Nerves showed up on his neck. His eyebrows crossed and his eyes rained blood. Mica spun and threw his dagger at Arthur's shoulder. Arthur grunted. Mica bent down and threw his dagger on the ground. The dagger rebounded and stabbed Arthur on his other shoulder. Mica ran and spun a kick on both of Arthur's shoulders and the dagger dug deep in. Arthur fell on his knee. Mica punched Arthur in the face. Mica tried pulling out the daggers. Arthur was in great pain. Arthur took a compass out from his pocket and stabbed it right on Mica's injured nose. Mica fell beside Arthur. Arthur took the compass out from Mica's nose. Mica pushed Arthur and took the daggers out from his shoulders. Mica kicked Arthur and sat again on him. But this time, Arthur couldn't do anything. Mica stuck both arms of Arthur on the ground with his dagger. " Goodbye, you were a good enemy," Mica said. He took another dagger from his pocket and lifted it to stab it in Arthur's chest. But death didn't want Arthur yet. Joel punched Mica away from Arthur. The detectives were there. " You thought we would let you die, huh?" Trent said opening his medical box." Trent, take care of Arthur. We'll take care of this," Priter said. " I didn't expect this many people. I think I'll need some reinforcement," Mica said, raising his hand. And this time nothing happened." Seems like I'm out of stock," Mica said, giving a nervous chuckle. Joel ran towards Mica and punched him. Martin kicked Mica in the stomach. Ivan slapped Mica in his ears. Toy punched Mica on the nose. Thud hit Mica with the batons." You didn't have guns. We didn't bring them too," Thud said. Priter held his hands. Joel held his head.

Scott had opened the door for the ol' guy. But there was no one outside. The light had gone suddenly. Scott was petrified. And the next moment, Scott was tied to a chair in the hall. The hall was lit up with a red bulb. Pill had reached there but the door was locked. So he went to the window and looked inside. The old guy that Scott had seen was inside and said," Hello Scott. Thank you very much." Scott replied," How do you know my name? Who are you?" The guy sat beside him and said," I am your boss. Oh! You won't understand. Well, how 'bout I'm Trent and Joel's father, Karen. And in terms of I'm your boss, look at it." A screen appeared and it had a report of Scott Langs. The report read' Suffering from Dissociative Identity Disorder.' Pill's mouth opened with shock. Karen continued," And you know, it's not shocking. But more shocking is this." The screen appeared again and this time Scott was in Mica's clothes. He was Scott and he was Mica." Shut up. You know everyone else is fighting Mica," Scott said. Karen replied," Well, he's the fake one. Have you ever seen him kill any civilian? I am Mica's boss. The riddle Priter solved in the cave, The game of the unsure, helped me get the cure for DID. Now listen, Trent was also suffering from DID. I was a doctor. I had created the medicine and had hidden it in the cave. Riots were going on and I didn't want the medicines to be demolished. One gets old, so I left clues so that someone could help me. And the bad things that happened with you were the things that you did yourselves. For example, when you were stabbed in the neck and were sitting in a taxi, you killed the driver. The driver hit the taxi to the bridge and the knife got away from your hand and stabbed you in the neck." Karen kept a syringe with red liquid in it in his hand and said," This can remove the Scott from you and leave the Mica in you. The fake Mica just had the reason right." Karen stabbed the syringe in Scott's arm. Scott closed his eyes and opened them again. This time his eyes had Mica's aggression, not Scott's politeness. Pill took his talkie out and said," Hey guys, you won't believe what I am seeing right now." His voice got lighter." Scott, my bestie, had Dissociative Identity Disorder. He was the real Mica. And, and, the boss, it's your father, Karen. He has treated Scott completely. We shouldn't let, let them leave. The Mica you're dealing with is fake." But Trent's talkie was already broken. As he heard about Scott, he dropped his talkie. The conversation was heard by everyone. Everyone left what they were doing with their eyes adrift. Fake Mica took advantage and took the batons and hit everyone in the head. They all fell down to the ground. They had blood coming out from their hairs. They were all unconscious but still, Trent dropped a tear that shined from the sunlight coming from the pipe they had slid down from.

Epilogue

So, guys, I think that's it for today. I'll come some other day and continue on this topic. Well, yeah, that's one of the most disturbing cases I've ever solved. Hey, Opium, you look a bit confused, what happened?

Yes, Sir, I'm Opium. And I'm confused because you haven't appeared a single time in this case.

Yes Opium, I will come later. It's the first day. We are detectives. And how I and my friends witnessed it, I'll tell later, when we'll continue the topic. Let's go on our patrol guard.

About The Author

Akshit[pet name, Mino Plants] has written his first ever novella. So not much to say. It took him 1 month to write the whole book. Well, he's sitting beside me and I'm his editor and he says he doesn't like to waste pages. So to talk more, visit

www.ingramcontent.com/pod-product-compliance
Lightning Source LLC
Chambersburg PA
CBHW031417160726
47993CB00003B/1272